The Snow Queen

Level 4

Retold by Audrey McIlvain

Series Editors: Annie Hughes and Melanie Williams

Pearson Education Limited
Edinburgh Gate, Harlow,
Essex CM20 2JE, England
and Associated Companies throughout the world.

ISBN 0582 430992

First published by Librairie du Liban Publishers, 1996
This adaptation first published 2000 under licence by
Penguin Books
© 2000 Penguin Books Ltd
Illustrations © 1996 Librairie du Liban

1 3 5 7 9 10 8 6 4 2

Design by Wendi Watson
Illustrations by Claire Mumford

Printed in Scotland by Scotprint, Musselburgh

Published by Pearson Education Limited in association with
Penguin Books Ltd,
both companies being subsidiaries of Pearson Plc

For a complete list of the titles available in the Penguin Young Readers series
please write to your local Pearson Education office or to:
Marketing Department, Penguin Longman Publishing,
5 Bentinck Street, London W1M 5RN

Once upon a time there was an ugly, wicked troll. He had lots and lots of horrible children with teeth and nails as sharp as his. One day he sat them all around him and, holding a mirror, said,

'Look at this mirror. It's magic! I wonder if you can guess what's magic about it.'
'It makes everyone look just like us!' one of the children said.
'No, no,' said the troll, 'it's better than that. It can turn a nice person into a mean, nasty person or a warm, kind person into a cold, greedy person.'

'Oh, what fun!' said the troll children together. 'What can we do with it?'

'I've got an idea,' said the nastiest of the troll children. 'Let's see how many people we can make nasty and mean like us!'

So, the troll children picked up the mirror and started to carry it away. But suddenly the mirror broke and thousands of tiny pieces of glass fell to earth.

Now, what will happen?

If one piece of glass from the mirror touches someone they will be nasty and mean for the rest of their life.

Far, far away in Denmark there lived two happy children, a girl called Gerda and her brother Kay. They were the best of friends as well as being brother and sister and they did everything together. Every day during the summer, they played in the fields and explored the countryside close to their grandmother's house.

Sometimes they went as far as the mountains, almost a day's walk away. They loved the animals at their grandmother's, especially the reindeer, Ned. The most fun they had was when they rode around on his back together.

When they felt hungry, they called down to
their grandmother from outside their bedroom
window.
'Hey, Granny! What's for tea today?'
And their grandmother would answer,
'Come down and see what's for tea, children!'

Often Kay would pick a red rose from outside
the window as a present for his grandmother.
He would hold it behind his back and then
surprise her with it at the last minute.
'Ta-rah! For you, beautiful lady!'
His grandmother was always surprised and
laughed and laughed. They were
such happy days for everyone.

In the winter when it was snowing and the snow was already deep outside, they would all sit by the lovely, warm fire. Their grandmother would make them hot chocolate and delicious cake and, with the cat sleeping on her lap, she would tell them stories. Granny's stories were of magic and mystery and far-away places.

'Once upon a time there was a Snow Queen who lived in a land of ice and snow…'

'Wow!'
'Go on…'

This was the best bit of the day for Kay and Gerda as their grandmother always told fantastic stories.

She was
a cold, hard queen
with no love in her heart.
Her face was cruel and
she never, never smiled.

'She always wore white like the snow, a white
hat, a white coat and boots. She didn't wear
gloves and, if you touched her hands, you
would find that they were as cold as her heart.
She would drive her sleigh through the falling
snow, silently passing by houses and villages.
People didn't see her but they would often say
to each other as she passed,
'"Ooh, What was that? I suddenly feel so cold."'

One winter's day Gerda and Kay were playing outside in the snow. They worked all day to build a snowman. At last it was finished.

'It looks great,' said Gerda. 'I like your green scarf and that funny, old hat we found in granny's house!'

'Ouch!' said Kay, 'I've got something in my eye. It really hurts.'

'Let me have a look,' said Gerda. 'I can't see anything, perhaps it was a piece of snow.'

But, it was not snow that was in Kay's eye, it was a piece of glass from the magic mirror.

Now, what will happen?

In one second Kay changed from a nice, kind person into a mean, nasty, horrible person. He suddenly grabbed his sledge and started to walk away from Gerda.

'I'm not playing with you any more, you silly girl,' he shouted at his sister.

'I'm going. Good-bye,' he said.

'But why? What's wrong?' asked Gerda.

Kay did not answer, but walked off towards the trees.

Gerda walked home alone, feeling very sad. 'Why did Kay shout at me?' she thought. 'Why?'

Suddenly, Kay heard a sound behind him and then a strange, cold voice. He turned round to look as a magical white sleigh came into view, driven by a tall lady dressed all in white.
'Faster, faster, you stupid horses,' she shouted, turning the whip high in the air.
There she was, the Snow Queen herself, in a beautiful white sleigh pulled by four white horses.
How hard and cruel her face looked as she shouted at the horses,
'Faster, faster.'

Kay stood still and watched, mouth open, as the Snow Queen stood up in her sleigh and whipped the horses. Again and again the whip fell.

'Faster, you stupid horses, faster,' she shouted.

'Is she crazy?' Kay thought as he watched. 'I don't think they could go any faster than that – but why not whip them? I love the sound the whip makes.'

The horses were galloping as fast as lightning now. Could they really go any faster?

You see, Kay was a mean, nasty, horrible person now and he liked watching the Snow Queen whipping the horses. Perhaps he was a little crazy too!

As the horses got closer and closer to the icy lake, they began to slow down. Kay waited for his chance and, when the sleigh was near, he threw the rope of his sledge over the back of the sleigh. The rope caught hold, he jumped onto the sledge just in time and he was OFF.

Off they went like lightning as the horses galloped over the icy lake.
'Stop! Stop!' he cried.

The sleigh started to slow down and at last it
stopped. The Snow Queen turned round and
looked straight into Kay's eyes.

'And who are you?' she said in her hard, cold,
cruel voice.

'My name's K...K...Kay. I w...w...wanted a
ride.'

'Enjoying it are you? Is it fast enough
for you?' the Snow Queen laughed
to herself. Then she was silent.
Finally she said, 'Come here,
quickly, sit beside me in
the sleigh.'

Kay was frightened
and got off his sledge and
into the sleigh beside her.
His heart was beating
faster and faster. What was
going to happen now?

Off they went across the snow like lightning.
Kay was so terrified that he could not speak.
He sat in the sleigh watching the trees race by.
'Faster, faster, you stupid horses,' the Snow
Queen shouted. She cracked the whip again
and again.

Crack. Crack. Crack. Crack.

Kay looked up at her. Her face was white and
her eyes looked like black ice, shining in the
dark night.

He was now a long, long way from his
happy, warm home where he knew
Gerda and his grandmother would
be waiting for him.

He was right. There in the little house, Gerda and his grandmother were waiting for him to come home. Gerda began to get frightened when he did not return and cried and cried for her brother. 'Where is he, Granny,' she asked. 'Where can he be? Why doesn't he come home? What can have happened to him?'

'I don't know my love,' said her grandmother. 'But I'm sure he's safe and he'll come home to us one day. I know he will.'

Gerda and her grandmother hugged each other and waited.

But Gerda cried and cried every day.
Kay never came.

One day, when she was tired of crying, she
picked a red rose from outside the bedroom
window.
'Granny,' she said, 'I can't
stay here and just wait.
I'm going to look for
my brother. I must find
Kay. Perhaps he needs
my help. I'll take this red
rose to him. I know it's
his favourite.'
'Oh Gerda, do be careful!'
her grandmother said.
'It's a dangerous world out
there. You don't know
what could happen.
You must take care of
yourself.'

Gerda collected a few clothes and some food together and put them in a small bag. She went down to the lake near the house and climbed into the little boat her grandmother kept there. She waved goodbye to her grandmother as the boat moved off into the lake.

She wanted to cry. Her heart was full of sadness and she felt small and very, very lonely. But, she was not frightened now. She was going to find Kay.

'I must be brave. I must do this. Oh Kay, where are you?'

After many days and nights in the little boat, Gerda knew that she was far from home. She had no idea where she was and she was very, very tired and hungry.

Suddenly she saw a little old lady standing by the lake, waving at her. Next to her was a pretty cottage and a garden full of flowers. How beautiful it all looked.

'Oh, you poor thing,' the old lady said. 'Come here and rest. You look thin and tired. Come and stay here with me for a while.'

Gerda gave the old lady the rope and they tied it to the gate of the cottage. Gerda was so tired she almost could not get out of the boat which had been her home for so long.

'My name is Alice,'
the old lady said in
a kind voice. 'Let me help
you out of the boat. I'll make
you something to eat and then you can
go to bed and sleep as long as you like.'
Oh, thank you,' said Gerda; 'you are so kind.
You have saved my life.'

Gerda went into the house with Alice. She had
something to eat and then slept and slept. She
was so tired she slept for twelve hours.

When she woke up, Alice cooked her a lovely
breakfast which tasted better then anything she
remembered. After breakfast she got dressed in
clean clothes – Alice had washed them for her
while she was asleep – and then Alice brushed
her hair for her.

'Oh Alice,' Gerda said; 'Will I find my brother?'
'Of course you will my dear. After a few days'
rest you'll feel strong and ready to go on.'

After three days Gerda felt much stronger and full of hope again. She said goodbye to Alice and thanked her for being so kind.

Gerda set off into the forest, on her journey to find Kay.
Kerrawk! Kerrawk!
What was that sound?
She heard it again. *'Kerrawk. Kerrawk'.*
Gerda looked up and saw a huge, black bird.
It landed in front of her.

'Come on little girl,' it said. 'The forest is no place for you. It's a dangerous place. Get on my back. Where do you want to go?'
'I'm looking for my brother,' Gerda said.
'What does your brother look like?' said the crow.

'He's small, with blond hair and blue eyes and
he has a yellow scarf,' said Gerda.
'Kerrawk. Kerrawk,' said the crow;
'I know where he is.'
'You do,' said Gerda,
'that's fantastic,
can we go there right now?'
'Of course,' said the crow.

The bird took Gerda to a castle
where a boy with blond hair and
blue eyes had just married a princess.
But … no … it was not Kay.
Gerda was so sad she thought her heart
would break.

23

The princess was very kind to Gerda.
'Take the reindeer,' she said, 'and go to
Sweden. My uncle is the king there and he'll
know what to do.'
So Gerda thanked her and set off again on the
reindeer.

It was a long journey and
they spent a night on a farm.

Gerda was tired but she could not sleep.
'Have you seen my brother, Kay?' she asked
the birds.
'Well, we saw a boy with the Snow Queen.
Perhaps it was him. Does he have a yellow
scarf?'
'Yes, oh yes! That's him. It must be!' said Gerda.

As soon as it was light Gerda set off again on the reindeer. She knew it was going to be a long, cold journey to find the Snow Queen. After travelling for many days, she met an old lady who lived in a tent at the edge of an icy lake.

'Do you know where the Snow Queen lives?' Gerda asked.
'It's far from here. You must go north, all the way to Finland,' she said pointing to the mountains.
'Then you must ask again. But be very careful. That woman is dangerous,' she said.

Gerda felt very tired and she was cold right through to her bones. When she cried her teardrops turned to ice.

They came, at last, to a tiny house in the middle of a forest where an old woman lived.
'Where is the Snow Queen? She has my brother,' Gerda said.
'You must go to the palace, it's not far from here,' said the old woman. 'But be careful, the Snow Queen has a heart of ice. She is a dangerous woman.'
Gerda ran off towards the palace, her heart beating like a drum.
'I must find him,' she said.

The Snow Queen was in
her palace of ice with Kay
as her prisoner.
'I have to go away for a while.
But you will stay here in
my palace. You are mine
for ever,' she told him.

Kay was cold, frightened and very,
very unhappy. He did not like it there.

The Snow Queen left Kay alone in the palace
and set off on her sleigh, cracking the whip to
make the horses go faster and faster. Kay could
hear her laughing as the sleigh disappeared into
the night.

Not long after the Snow Queen had left, Gerda
arrived at the palace of ice.
'Oh, Kay you are safe!' she said.
'Who are you?' asked Kay. 'I don't know you.'
'You don't know me? I'm your sister. Oh Kay
look, I've brought a red rose for you. It's from
Granny's garden.'

Gerda started to cry as she spoke and her
warm teardrops fell onto Kay's face. They
washed the tiny piece of glass from Kay's eye.
THEN – he remembered.
'Oh, Gerda. We are in great danger. We must
go quickly before the Snow Queen comes
back,' he said.

They ran out of the palace and back to the tiny
house where Gerda had left the reindeer with
the old woman. She was happy that Gerda had
found her brother but knew they were in danger.
'Quickly' she said, 'you must leave.'

They jumped onto the
reindeer's back and
travelled back to Denmark
as fast as they could.

'Oh, my dear children,' said their grandmother
when she saw them. 'I can't believe you're safe
again,' and she hugged them both.
'Let's have some hot chocolate and cake and
then we can have a story.'

So, they sat down together beside the lovely warm fire with their hot chocolate and delicious cake to hear one of their grandmother's stories of magic and mystery and far-away places.

It was just as if they had never been away.

Then Kay said to his grandmother,
'Granny, can you tell us a story about a warm, kind, happy Snow Queen this time?'
They all laughed and then their grandmother began to tell them a story.

Activities

Before you read

1. Look at the cover of the book.
   Do you think the story will be:

 sad   happy

 funny   frightening?

   Tick (✔) the one you think is right.

2. Treasure Hunt
   Look in the book for pages with pictures of:

   a sledge   a red rose   a rope   a troll
   a whip   a sleigh   a reindeer   a mirror

   Use your dictionary if you need to

3. Find out the names of the boy and the girl in the story. Write them down here.

Activities

After you read

1. Use your atlas, a map or a globe to find these countries:

   Denmark

   Sweden

   Finland

   Which country do you think the Snow Queen lived in?

2. True ✔ or False ✗
   a) The Snow Queen was happy and kind.
   b) Gerda was very brave.
   c) Granny made delicious cakes.
   d) Kay was frightened of the Snow Queen.
   e) Gerda spent the night in a garden.
   f) Kay wore a green scarf.

3. What do you think the Snow Queen did when she got back to the palace after Kay had left?